For Pedro, my little bird

Translation copyright © 2014 by Random House Children's Books

All rights reserved. Published in the United States by Schwartz & Wade Books,
an imprint of Random House Children's Books, a division of Random House LLC,
a Penguin Random House Company, New York. Originally published in France as
J'ai un Ours by Éditions Gallimard Jeunesse, Paris, France, in 2011.
Copyright © 2011 by Éditions Gallimard Jeunesse

Schwartz & Wade Books and the colophon are trademarks of Random House LLC.

Visit us on the Web! randomhouse.com/kids

Educators and librarians, for a variety of teaching tools, visit us at
RHTeachersLibrarians.com

Library of Congress Cataloging-in-Publication Data
Ruiz Johnson, Mariana, author, illustrator.
[J'ai un ours. English]
I know a bear / Mariana Ruiz Johnson.—First American edition.
pages cm
Summary: Each time a girl visits a bear in a zoo, she listens to his tales of
the vast and wondrous Land of the Bears, his home that he will never see again.
ISBN 978-0-385-38614-2 (hc) — ISBN 978-0-385-38615-9 (glb) —
ISBN 978-0-385-38616-6 (ebook)
[1. Listening—Fiction. 2. Bears—Fiction. 3. Zoo animals—Fiction.] I. Title.
PZ7.R8867Iak 2014
[E]—dc23
2013046706

The text of this book is set in Odetta.
The illustrations were rendered in graphite pencil and finished in Adobe Photoshop.
Book design by Rachael Cole

MANUFACTURED IN CHINA
2 4 6 8 10 9 7 5 3 1
First American Edition

I Know a Bear

Mariana Ruiz Johnson

schwartz & wade books · new york

I know a bear
that comes from far away.

From a place he calls
the Land of the Bears.

He tells me
that the
breakfasts
there are
sweet,

the trails are lush,

and the rivers are
like bathtubs.

Naps last for months
and months.

This is what
he tells me.

The bear tells me
that this place
is both

vast and wondrous.

But
he
cannot
go
back
there.

That's why each time
I visit him,

I listen carefully
as he remembers.

Today I had an idea.

It felt both vast

and wondrous.